GHOULIA

GHOULIA

AND THE DOOMED MANOR

Book 4

Text and illustrations by Barbara Cantini
Translated from the Italian by Anna Golding

Amulet Books
New York

Cataloging-in-Publication Data has been applied for and may be obtained from the Library of Congress.

ISBN 978-1-4197-5003-8

Text and illustrations by Barbara Cantini
Original Italian title: *Mortina e la vacanza al Lago Mistero*
© 2019 Mondadori Libri S.p.A.
Translation by Anna Golding
Art Director for original Ghoulia series: Fernando Ambrosi
Graphic Designer for original Ghoulia series: Stefano Moro
Page 42 image courtesy chippix / shutterstock.com

Book design by Jade Rector

Printed and bound in China
10 9 8 7 6 5 4 3 2 1

Amulet Books are available at special discounts when purchased in quantity for premiums and promotions as well as fundraising or educational use. Special editions can also be created to specification. For details, contact specialsales@abramsbooks.com or the address below.

ABRAMS The Art of Books
195 Broadway, New York, NY 10007
abramsbooks.com

This book is dedicated to all my young fans. It is very unlikely that, without your enthusiasm, this book would have been written.

I would like to thank the editorial team at Mondadori Children's Books for continuing to work so hard to make this series such a success. A particular thank you to everyone who is close to me and, once again, to Francesco Maria Petrini, for his invaluable help with the Latin.

Look out for a hidden "thank you" in the pages of the book.
—B. C.

The Residents of

GHOULIA

AUNTIE DEPARTED

TRAGEDY

SHADOW

Crumbling Manor

ROTTEN

UNCLE MISFORTUNE

GRANDAD COFFIN

The Residents of

AUNTIE WITCH

DILBERT

Fancy Manor

MAYHEM

DANGER

BARTIMEUS

One morning, the residents of Crumbling Manor woke to the ringing of the old telephone. Auntie Departed was very grouchy until she recognized the voice on the other end of the line.

BRRIIIING!

It was her sister, Auntie Witch. She was calling to invite them all to visit her and Cousin Dilbert at Fancy Manor, on the shores of Lake Mystery. She wanted to celebrate the summer solstice together—especially because, that year, it coincided with the Great Red Moon. It was a rare and exciting event!

Great Uncle Misfortune used to go there on holiday as a boy. He explained that on the night of the Great Red Moon, the waters had mysterious powers . . . but was it really true?

Detachable ears mean easy eavesdropping!

Ghoulia had never been to Fancy Manor before,
and she wasn't very excited about seeing Dilbert again.
But she did like the idea of going on *vacation*!

She hadn't been anywhere farther than
the village in maybe . . . thirty years?!

Three days later, they were ready to leave.

Grandad Coffin's old ice-cream truck (there is nothing better than a chilled compartment to maintain Auntie's wrinkles!)

The family set off together for Lake Mystery. Tragedy, the albino greyhound, was their driver.

Uncle Misfortune grumbled that they should have left at night, but Auntie Departed had wanted to do it the way living folks did: "We set off at dawn, even if we are dead."

Repainted so that no children approach for ice-cream

Blacked-out windows to avoid being seen

After several hours of travel up and down mountains and around winding paths, they finally arrived at Fancy Manor.

Fancy Manor

Lake Mystery

Lord Otto,
a friend of
Auntie Witch

Dilbert,
the pack mule

Auntie Witch and Dilbert
welcomed them at the door.
The aunties were overjoyed to see
each other again—they hadn't spent
time together since they were alive!

Dilbert tried to carry the guests' luggage
to their rooms, but he struggled up the grand
staircase. He was not exactly used to hard work.

After they had settled in, the family went down to the lake to enjoy the afternoon and take a dip. The aunties sunbathed while Dilbert showed off his diving skills. He got everyone's attention and then . . . he splashed clumsily into the water.

Dilbert reemerged covered in muddy weeds and missing an arm. Thankfully, Tragedy managed to track it down. (He's a much better swimmer than Dilbert.)

At that very moment, a car pulled up to the manor's gates. A serious and dull-looking man attached something to the railing.

Hiding and listening

After the car drove off, the family emerged
from their hiding spot and read the sign.

PROPERTY TO BE AUCTIONED

HOUSE IS CURRENTLY UNINHABITED

NO KNOWN LIVING HEIRS

The fine print read: *In the event of no legal heir making
themselves known at the town hall, the property will be
auctioned off this Friday.*

Auntie Witch flew into a total panic! Green sweat started dripping from her pores, and she changed from her usual grayish color to a pale shade of white.

They had to save the manor, but how?
After they came up with several absurd plans, it was Dilbert who finally suggested a real solution.

ZOMBIE PANIC: SIGNS OF DISORDER AND DISTRESS

MAIN SYMPTOM:

GREEN SWEAT

1. Acquire a glass jar.

2. Collect droplets of the green sweat from panicked elderly zombie.

3. Dab on face as necessary to achieve splendid warts.

Very fashionable among the zombie community ←

SECONDARY SYMPTOMS:

WHITER THAN A GHOST:
When a zombie panics, she turns very, very pale. She appears even whiter than her closest undead friend—the ghost.

— ACNE —

Dilbert ran home immediately and returned with an old book:
THE LAWS AND LEGENDS OF LAKE MYSTERY.

He was well acquainted with this book and immediately
turned to the page titled "The Back-to-Life Potion."

PROPERTY TO BE
AUCTIONED

HOUSE IS CURRENTLY
UNINHABITED

NO KNOWN
LIVING HEIRS

Uncle
Misfortune
hitched a ride.

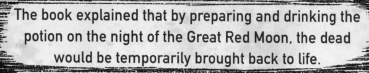

The book explained that by preparing and drinking the potion on the night of the Great Red Moon, the dead would be temporarily brought back to life.

THE BACK-TO-LIFE POTION

On the eve of the shortest night lit up by the bloodred full moon, collect Magic Mint, and you will be able to brew a Back-to-Life potion.

What You Will Need:

5 wake-me-up flowers, 7 lively pistils, 3 scampering roots, 3 high-spirited berries, 3 stubborn roots, 1 clove of garlic. Grind everything with a pestle and mortar and boil at midnight on the eve of the summer solstice for 7 minutes under the light of the Great Red Moon. Before drinking, repeat 3 times:

"CARMINA POSSUNT DEDUCERE LUNAM"

The others gazed at Dilbert in disbelief, and Auntie Witch declared that it was all a load of nonsense. However, Ghoulia backed Dilbert up immediately. They should be prepared to try anything, and time was slipping away.

In order to get some Magic Mint, they would need to reach the little island in the middle of the lake that very evening. At dusk, Ghoulia, Dilbert, and Tragedy set sail. They collected the Magic Mint and brought it back home to brew the potion.

At the stroke of midnight, they started to brew the potion. They made a whole cauldron full, just in case. The most important thing was to ensure there was enough for Auntie Witch. She would go to the village and prove she was the rightful owner of the manor.

When it was time to drink the potion, Auntie Witch was so panicked that she almost didn't agree to go through with it. But Ghoulia offered to drink it with her—she would come back to life, too!

They drank it all up in one go! Then they waited . . . and waited . . .

And absolutely nothing happened!

Auntie Witch was at her wit's end. "Dilbert," she said, "this was a completely ridiculous idea!"

She then stomped off to bed swearing that, no matter what happened, she wouldn't go back to living in the cemetery. "Over my dead body!" she screamed before slamming the door.

Exhausted and worried, the rest of the family trooped off to bed, hopeful that a good night's sleep meant they would have a better idea tomorrow.

The whole manor awoke the next morning to a delighted shriek. Auntie Witch was staring at her reflection in the grand mirror. She had pink skin, soft hair, and none of her limbs could be removed. The potion had worked!

"Oh my goodness! I look gorgeous!" said Auntie Witch.

Spiky thistles from Lake Mystery

Danger and Mayhem

Auntie Witch's feather boa

Meanwhile, a sleepy Ghoulia padded down the stairs, still in her pajamas.

Two of Auntie Witch's husbands

"What's going on?" she asked.

Everyone turned to look at Ghoulia and gasped!

Ghoulia ran to the mirror. A girl with glowing red cheeks and shiny black hair stared back at her, speechless. She felt so   alive!

Tragedy brought everyone back to reality by pointing out that fashions had changed in the last fifty years. Everyone would need to update their wardrobes.

WOW!

He also reminded Auntie Witch to change her date of birth that was included in the paperwork for the manor. Nobody would believe that she was more than

Waiting nervously . . .

Once they were ready, Tragedy drove Ghoulia and Auntie Witch to the town hall in the ice-cream truck.

Auntie Witch was nervous, but she walked right in and introduced herself. She said that there had been a mistake—she was the legal owner of Fancy Manor and felt more alive than ever!

She explained this all with a sweet smile, fluttering her thick new eyelashes.

Bored to death

The town planner continued to cite an endless list
of ridiculous laws, almost causing Ghoulia and her auntie
to die once again of sheer boredom.

Finally, he said, "I believe that everything is in order!"
He then added, blushing, "I imagine that you will be staying here
at the lake for a few days. May I ask where you are residing?"

Without a moment's thought, Auntie Witch replied,
"Oh, at the manor, with my family!"

The town planner looked a little confused; the house seemed to be in a state of total disrepair. And—in accordance with Article number 637, subsection circle-slash-diamond—not up to health and safety codes!

Auntie Witch tried to reassure him, saying that although the house *looked* a wreck from the outside, inside everything was fine. She also told him that she adored the "shabby chic" look, but he was insistent. Tomorrow he would come by for tea to check on the house and deem whether it was fit to live in.

Oh no!

Once back at Fancy Manor, everyone was ready to celebrate, but Auntie Witch put the festivities on hold. They had to completely tidy up the house, and *everybody* would need to return to life for tomorrow's visitor. The whole family was very anxious. However, Tragedy took charge of coordinating the cleanup operation.

Dilbert is horrified by the idea of having to clean!

Uncle Misfortune began dusting with a little help from Rotten.

Vital support

Ghoulia, along with Auntie Departed, touched up some paint here and there.

Dilbert mopped the floors.

Auntie Witch polished her antique tea set and dug out an ancient recipe book for living beings. She wanted to bake cookies to serve with the tea.

That evening, before bedtime, the family had a toast
to drink up the remaining potion. They hoped that
everything would go according to plan the following day.

The next morning, everyone looked splendidly . . . alive!

Dilbert as a young boy

The tea club hosted by Granny Coffin

Iced tea to toast with

The next day, at five o'clock on the dot, the town planner's car parked in front of Fancy Manor.

Ghoulia's family, alive and very tense, was ready to receive their visitor. The only person missing from the welcome party was Uncle Misfortune, who—given his lack of a body—risked provoking some awkward questions.

They greeted their guest in the living room, where Auntie Departed was on hand to serve tea and cookies to everyone. Against his wishes, Tragedy played the role of a pet dog, and Auntie Witch introduced Dilbert and Ghoulia as her children.

Before tea was to be served, the planner inspected the house. He appreciated the rich antique furnishings and decor, but noted that the stairwell needed some work in accordance with Article 234 in relation to the horizontal and vertical rules on safety . . .

Bartimeus in disguise

. . . and the roof, plumbing, and wiring all needed to be fixed in accordance with Article number 344, line 6, remainder 2. After which, satisfied with how the inspection had gone, he shuffled back down to the ground floor.

As the town planner made his way downstairs, he noticed that sticking out from behind a plant on the landing was . . . a HEAD! It was nosy old Uncle Misfortune! Flabbergasted, the man pointed to the head, and Auntie Witch quickly grabbed it, saying, "Oh, that's just one of my handbags! You know that I have quite a quirky sense of style."

The town planner was startled but reassured,
so he continued his tour of the house.

But once they arrived back in the living room,
the magic potion started to lose its power.

After the inspection, everyone sat down for tea. A black spider crept out of the sleeve of Auntie Departed's dress—it crawled over her hand, which had turned a grayish-purple color, and wandered over the tablecloth. The man caught only a quick glance before Auntie Departed speedily caught the spider and scooped it away.

Next, Dilbert's appearance started to falter. His arm, only just restitched after the accident at the lake, was starting to tear off again after he carried the tray of cookies.

Thank goodness Rotten is on hand to resew . . .

Auntie Witch tried to distract the town planner from Dilbert's limb, but then Ghoulia's face returned to its usual pale color with purple shadows under her eyes. The man, rather worried, wanted to rush her to hospital, but Ghoulia reassured him by saying that she was only suffering a tummy ache, probably caused by eating too many sweets.

To wrap up their little party, Auntie Witch announced that she had to leave immediately. The visit finished in the nick of time, a horrific experience both because it was so anxiety-inducing and *so boring*!

Once the town planner was gone, everyone breathed a deep sigh of relief. It had been a fun adventure to return to life for a bit, but ultimately, they were all delighted to be dead again!

A costume party in 1887

Cousin McDeath posing (and some skinny guy on the left)

"Do you know what I think?" said Ghoulia.
"Better to be dead on the outside than dead on the inside!"

Turn the page for some
extra-special fun!

Auntie Witch's Back-to-Life Potion!

A minty lemonade so tasty, it might just raise the dead!

INGREDIENTS

6 lemons
4 cups of water
Sugar or honey (about 1 cup)
A handful of fresh mint leaves
Ice

Step 1: Wash your hands!

Step 2: With the help of a grown-up, slice the lemons in half and give each one a good squeeze. If you don't like pulp in your juice, you can pour it through a strainer.

Step 3: Mix the lemon juice and water together.

Step 4: Add honey or sugar to taste.

Step 5: Rip the mint leaves away from the stem, leaving the leaves whole. Stir the mint into the lemonade.

Step 6: Refrigerate for one hour.

Step 7: Serve over ice. Cheers!

Dilbert's Word Search

Help Dilbert find his family members to help him with his mission to brew the Back-to-Life potion!

```
C  S  R  U  U  Y  C  Y  D  W  O  L  E  K  V
Z  M  A  U  N  T  I  E  W  I  T  C  H  U  A
J  A  U  N  T  I  E  D  E  P  A  R  T  E  D
T  Q  P  G  K  R  C  I  C  Y  D  L  J  R  Q
M  H  P  R  B  M  Y  B  U  F  R  G  G  D  U
R  G  Z  P  M  Z  U  U  U  U  H  P  H  A  W
U  N  C  L  E  M  I  S  F  O  R  T  U  N  E
K  M  V  Q  H  T  S  A  N  Y  C  R  P  G  G
K  A  J  X  Z  R  O  T  T  E  N  A  G  E  H
Q  Y  X  D  W  D  K  A  M  V  Y  G  M  R  O
J  H  B  A  R  T  I  M  E  U  S  E  S  A  U
N  E  Q  V  X  M  Q  E  U  L  G  D  F  B  L
U  M  G  A  M  W  V  M  A  P  I  Y  F  P  I
E  O  S  F  E  E  N  H  O  L  E  Q  H  F  A
G  V  R  V  M  O  E  Z  X  Y  E  F  Q  W  E
```

Ghoulia	Uncle Misfortune	Bartimeus
Auntie Departed	Tragedy	Danger
Auntie Witch	Rotten	Mayhem

Decorate your own haunted house!

Complete Fancy Manor with
lots of fun and spooky details!

Collect all of Ghoulia's adventures!